LITTLE SOUP'S BIRTHDAY

OTHER YOUNG YEARLING BOOKS
YOU WILL ENJOY

YEARLING BOOKS / YOUNG YEARLINGS / YEARLING CLASSICS are designed especially to entertain and enlighten young people. Patricia Reilly Giff, consultant to this series, received her bachelor's degree from Marymount College and a master's degree in history from St. John's University. She holds a Professional Diploma in Reading and a Doctorate of Humane Letters from Hofstra University. She was a teacher and reading consultant for many years, and is the author of numerous books for young readers.

For a complete listing of all Yearling titles, write to Dell Readers Service, P.O. Box 1045, South Holland, IL 60473.

LITTLE SOUP'S BIRTHDAY

Robert Newton Peck

Illustrated by Charles Robinson

A YOUNG YEARLING BOOK

Published by
Dell Publishing
a division of
Bantam Doubleday Dell Publishing Group, Inc.
666 Fifth Avenue
New York, New York 10103

The trademark Yearling® is registered in the U.S. Patent and Trademark Office.

The trademark Dell® is registered in the U.S. Patent and Trademark Office.

ISBN: 0-440-40551-3

Printed in the United States of America

December 1991

10 9 8 7 6 5 4 3 2

CWO

LITTLE SOUP'S BIRTHDAY

One

"Robert." Someone was calling
my name. But I really didn't want to
listen up. Why not? Because I was

asleep. And not only that, but also having a nice dream.

In the dream, it was my birthday. There was a big birthday cake, brightly frosted. Sparkling with candles. Beside the cake lay my present. A red sled. It had two steel runners. They were both silver, and shining.

"Robert, wake up. It's chore time."

This wasn't the voice of anyone in my dream.

I opened one eye. Again I heard my mother's voice. "Robert, it's almost five o'clock."

We lived on a farm. If you are a farmer, five o'clock in the morning means milking time. So does five o'clock in the evening. Twice a day. Every day. Even on my birthday.

But right now, it wasn't my birthday, because mine comes around the middle of February. Today, I knew, was still October. "It's Saturday," Mama told me. "And you know, Robert, how special this Saturday is."

I knew.

Pulling on a sock, I recalled that today was a very important day. Because today was Soup's birthday.

His real name was Luther Wesley Vinson. Mine was Robert Newton Peck. The pair of us were next-farm neighbors. And best pals. We lived in Vermont.

Almost everybody here was a farmer. Or a farmer's wife. Or maybe a farm kid. Or a farm animal. Or a bug.

"Rob, do you know what today is?" Mama shouted up the stairs.

Pulling on a boot, another boot, then a flannel shirt and a wool sweater, I answered my mother. "I sure do, Mama. It's Soup's birthday. And I don't guess I can wait to go to Soup's birthday party." My fingers scratched my long woolen underwear.

I went to the kitchen. Mama was looking out the window over the sink. It was still dark outside. "Snow," she said.

I looked out too. "Boy oh boy," I said, "our first snow of the winter. And it's only October."

My mother moaned.

Two

I ran out to the barn. The snow was still falling. Wet snow. So I stopped just long enough to pack a snowball. Inside the barn, I threw my snowball at Papa. And luckily missed. Even in winter (and late October is sometimes very close to being winter in Vermont) a cow barn is a warm place. Because of the cows.

We kept Holsteins. Their big black-and-white bodies made our barn very warm. Even at five o'clock in the morning, before the sun was up. Papa often called our cows *hay burners.* I helped my father with chores and milking.

In warm weather, our cows stayed outside all night. But not in cold snowy weather. Last night they stayed in the barn. This made our chores take longer. More shovel work.

We finally finished. Papa and I returned to the house, to wash up. Papa walked. I waded. The snow was coming down a bit harder now. On the ground it sure was deeper. "Today is Soup's birthday," I told my father for the tenth time.

"Is that a fact," he said. It wasn't a question. Just his way to answer me. We ate breakfast. I ate the most. Even though I got up from the table with every mouthful to peek out the kitchen window. It gave me something to do while I chewed. Or swallowed.

"Snow's getting deeper," I said.

"Is that a fact," Mama answered, as though she could have said the words in her sleep.

In the winter, snow is really no big surprise to a Vermonter. We're ready for it. Then it comes. We shovel.

But I didn't complain about having to help Papa. Snow is clean to shovel. And almost fun.

Three

Knock.
I stopped eating.
Knock. Knock.
Even though it wasn't yet seven

o'clock in the morning, and snowing, somebody was knocking at our kitchen door.

Knock. Knock. Knock.

"It's Soup," I said quickly, jumping up from the kitchen table where we always ate. "I'm going to help him plan the party."

"At this hour?" Mama asked.

I opened the door for my best pal. In marched Luther Wesley Vinson. Soup's cheeks were cherry red, his nose was running, and his boots were frosted with fresh snow.

He looked like a cherry sundae.

Mama made him remove his boots and placed them on an old raggy rug behind our big black cooking stove. Soup smiled.

"Guess what today is," he said, wiggling a green-socked foot at us.

Papa groaned. "Christmas," he said.

"Easter," said Mama.

Soup Vinson shook his head. "No, it's my birthday."

"Well, I'll be," said Papa. "This certain is one heck of a big surprise."

"Guess how old I am," Soup said, coming to the kitchen table to join us.

"Eighty," said Mama.

"Six weeks," said Papa.

Soup laughed. "Today, I'm *nine.*"

"Is that a fact."

Soup was a year and four months older than I was. Right now, I was almost coming up eight. My birthday was February seventeenth. For me, this was a perfect month. Because I planned to become famous like George Washington and Abraham Lincoln, also born in February.

Soup munched a hot biscuit that Mama fixed for him. I ate one too. Then he ate another one.

"A year from today," Soup said with his mouth full, "I'll turn ten. And that means I'll final have two numbers to my age, instead of just one."

"Yes," said Mama, pouring herself a second cup of hot steamy coffee from the pot, "and in only ninety-one more years, you'll have three numbers."

"Right," said Papa, "you'll be a century old."

I said, "You'll be one hundred."

Soup sighed. "I can't wait."

Four

_____

We went to my room.

"Okay," said Soup, "let's see your junk."

Both of us kept old beat-up shoeboxes under our beds. In secret hiding. I pulled out my box. Here's what lay under its lid:

1. Several long pieces of string.
2. Bits of string too short to save.
3. Three marbles (two were chipped).
4. A plugged-up harmonica that would only blow two squeaky notes.
5. Half of a golf ball.
6. A pair of busted drumsticks.
7. Five bottle caps, all bent.
8. A dried chicken wishbone.
9. A Mel Ott baseball card.
10. One cork fishing bobber, two rusty hooks, and a knotted line.
11. A faded photo of General Robert E. Lee.
12. And a dead toad.

"Rob," said Soup, "this is nifty stuff."

"It's all yours," I said, "because you said you'll need prizes for the party games, like Hog Pile and Rat Race."

"Thanks," said Soup. "You're a pal."

I picked up my toad. "He got run over out on the county road."

Soup said, "No wonder he's so flat."

It was true. He looked less like a toad and more like a waffle, due to the tire marks.

"Flat toads come in handy," I told him. "Because they're easy to slip into your pocket."

"Or," said Soup, "into your mother's purse."

Then, when Soup wasn't looking, I slipped the flat toad into my pocket.

Looking out of my window, I could see that it was teasing to be morning. Yet there was no sunrise. Only snow. The sky was a pewter gray, and misty, with millions and millions of snowflakes. They floated softly downward, six arms outstretched, an endless swarm of white butterflies.

Soup and I went outdoors to check on how deep the snow was piling. Six inches. Standing out in the storm, we tilted our heads back, and opened our mouths, to catch snowflakes on our tongues.

"Each one is different," said Soup.

"That's right. Miss Kelly told us that in school."

"She said no two snowflakes are the same, but all of them are hexagons."

Away up high, I spotted an extra-big flake. It was falling very slowly. Almost like a white parachute. "Look," I yelled to Soup. Mouth open, I ran beneath it, and let it land gently on my tongue.

It melted.

"Rob," said Soup, "you just ate a hexagon."

Back inside, Mama put both of us to work turning the handle of the ice cream machine. The flavor would be vanilla, she told us.

I could almost taste the ice cream. Vanilla! My favorite flavor.

Soup cranked around and around. Then I cranked. Clickety clickety clickety. Making ice cream isn't work. It's a winter sport.

Five

We went to Soup's house. With us, we took my box of prize junk, the present my mother made for Soup, and the silver freezer full of fresh ice cream. It was still morning. Still gray. And snowing very hard.

"It's mounting up deeper and deeper," Soup said.

I agreed. "It certain is. And, right now, it's maybe only ten o'clock."

"By noon," Soup told me, as we both used brooms to brush the snow and slush off our boots, "we might be up to our knees in hexagons."

Inside, Mrs. Vinson told me to thank my mother for the ice cream.

"I smell something," said Soup. He glanced at the oven.

"Out of my kitchen, both of you," Mrs. Vinson said, "because what's baking is none of your business." She winked. "Leastwise, not yet."

We left.

"It's a *cake*," Soup whispered. "For *us.*"

We went to Soup's room to think up a few games for his birthday party. I suggested Red Rover. But Soup quickly shook his head. "For some reason," he said, "my mother won't allow rough games in the house. Not after what happened to the lamp."

"Well," I said, "how about Hide the Thimble?"

"Good idea," said Soup. "It's a boring game. It doesn't ever smash anything." Soup put it down on a list. "We'll also try Pin the Tail on the Donkey."

We ruled out Crack the Whip because, like Tag, it could be a rough game and wreck a lot of lamps. The same for Red Rover.

"Soup," I said, "I just thought of a

great game to play at your party. But only if your mother thought to buy a bag of jelly beans."

He made a curious face. "Jelly beans?"

"Or gumdrops," I said.

"What's the name of the game?"

"String Chew," I told him.

"How do you play it?"

I smiled. "You'll soon see. I want to sort of save it for a surprise." I took a deep breath. "Because I couldn't buy you a birthday present."

Soup punched my shoulder in a friendly way. Not hard. And not hurtful.

"Rob, old sport, pals never have to buy presents for each other. It's enough just being a friend."

As I looked at Soup, I knew that I'd rather have one good pal with a box of junk than be alone with all the store toys in the world.

I figured Soup felt the same.

Six

"Rob," said Soup, "I've got some junk too."

"Where is it?"

Soup scratched his head. "That's

the problem. My box of stuff was so valuable that I hid it. But darn if I can't remember where."

"Under your bed?"

"No. That's where it used to be."

"Out in the cow barn?"

"No. Not there. I put my shoebox in a safe place. So safe that even I can't locate it." Soup's face lit up like a birthday candle. "Ah," he said, "it's up attic."

While I waited, Soup went scampering off to find it. He returned with a shoebox. And a smile.

"Wait until you take a look at this great stuff," said Soup. "It may look like junk to grown-ups. But remember, what's trash to parents is treasure to a kid."

My pal Soup was right. It was treasure. His beat-up shoebox was, to us, a pirate's chest of gems and jewels and priceless plunder.

One by one, Soup produced:

1. A sardine-can key.
2. An empty pop bottle which held a horseshoe nail and a bent penny.
3. A jackknife with one blade missing.
4. Half of the words for a baseball song we both liked to sing, called *Take Me out to the Ball Game.*
5. A picture of the greatest baseballer who ever played

the game. Tyrus Raymond
Cobb.

6. Seven gum wrappers that
   contained no gum, but still
   had a little bit of the
   smell. And some powder to
   lick.
7. A turkey foot.
8. One pencil, with no lead in
   it, but the wood had a lot of
   teethmarks.
9. Three horse chestnuts.
10. A red heart-shaped and
    perfume-drenched valentine
    from a girl who failed to
    sign her name.
11. Two Kellogg's Corn Flakes
    boxtops.

12. A small glass bottle filled with Soup's lifetime collection of dead spiders.

"Soup," I said, "this is super stuff. You're not going to give it all away as game prizes, are you?"

"No, not at *my* party. Rob, to tell you the truth, I'm saving it for *yours.*"

"Thanks," I said.

"And for you," he said, "I'll even wrap the turkey leg."

Soup's birthday party had been planned for two o'clock. Right now, it was only noon. I liked noon. It was my favorite time of day. Both clock hands were pointed straight up.

Noon was the only time I could tell.

Outside the snow was still falling. Perhaps we'd get too much of it. Yet I didn't want to mention this to Soup.

Mrs. Vinson fixed us both a rhubarb sandwich, and a cup of homemade pork-bone chowder. With a soda cracker on the side. It tasted great. And I told her so.

"Will two o'clock ever come?" Soup asked.

"Always has," Mrs. Vinson answered. Soup and I went outside to play in the snow.

We built a fort, and then we made a snowman. We used two lumps of coal for eyes, a carrot for a nose, and stuck Soup's father's pipe in its mouth. We named him Mr. Hexagon. Then, as a final touch, we tied a long rag around the snowman's neck to look like a scarf. Plus a scruffy hat. He looked like somebody's grandfather. Yet he wasn't even an hour old.

Seven

It never came.

The big snowplow never came at all. A few large trucks went by, all going downhill, loaded up high with spruce logs, headed for the paper mill in town. Nobody came uphill.

"The road's all covered," said Soup. "Nobody will be able to get up here from town. The road will be packed too slick."

Soup was right.

Their telephone rang. Soup's mother answered. We could tell that somebody couldn't come to the party. The phone kept on ringing. And ringing. Nobody would be coming. No one at all.

"Rob," said Soup, "we have to do something."

"Right," I told Soup, "and fast."

"Now," said Soup, "all we have to do is find our collection of old tennis racquets that we lugged home from the dump."

I looked out the window. "Tennis? In a snowstorm?"

"Yes," he said, "if we can also find those long strings of red licorice I was saving."

We found all we needed. Four tennis racquets, and licorice; so out into the white hexagons we went.

I still didn't know what Soup was

up to. Then I learned. What a surprise it was.

Using the long strings of red licorice, Soup tied a tennis racquet to the bottom of his boot. The handle pointed straight back.

"What is it?" I asked.

"Rob, can't you see? It's a snowshoe."

"Wow!"

Quickly we made three more. Two were now under Soup's boots. Two under mine. Over the deep snow we waded. Not very fast. But we got to Mr. McKell's house. We knocked on his door.

Mr. McKell answered. When he saw our funny snowshoes he laughed so hard that tiny sparks flew up out of his pipe. "Boys," he said, "I owe you both a favor. Because you gave me a good laugh. Whatever it is you want, I'll help you do it. If I can."

We told him. Crossing his fingers, Mr. McKell agreed to try. But said he couldn't promise because of all the bad weather.

Soup and I thanked him in advance, and waded through the snow, back to Soup's house. We took off our racquets and then ate the licorice.

We went inside. Soup had a collection of old mussed-up grocery bags. We used them to wrap our junk for party prizes. Just in case the snowstorm stopped. We pretended the brown bags were fancy wrapping paper. Our best bag said GRAND UNION on it.

When Soup wasn't looking, I wrapped a special surprise for him. I even made a little white bow, using pieces of string that were too short to save. It was lucky I'd saved them.

Soup, however, was still sad. After all, when you plan a birthday party, with games, and plenty of nifty prizes, it feels worse than a punch in the nose when nobody can come.

Soup looked at the clock. Then he sighed. "It's two o'clock," he said. I took his word for it. Because I looked at the clock too. All I could tell was that it sure wasn't noon. But then something happened. A big surprise. Soup and I heard a noise. It was a sound that I didn't expect to hear. Yet a very happy sound. Suddenly I was smiling. So was Soup.

Eight

"Wow," said Soup. "Hear that, Rob?"

"I sure do. It's bells."

A horse snorted. Both of us raced to the window. Sure enough, there was a horse and a sleigh, and five small boys jumping down from it and into the fresh snow. I knew who they were:

Ally Tidwell
Rolly McGraw
George Davis
Stevie Seguso
Karl Kopek

They were our five best buddies at school.

I was glad that Eddy Tacker wasn't coming, because Eddy was a bully who liked to knock other kids down. Even girls. Except for Janice Riker, who was the toughest kid in our school. Nobody messed with Janice. At least, nobody who was still alive.

Soup and I rushed downstairs and

to the front door, knocking each other down to see who would get there first. "Easy now," said Mrs. Vinson. I remembered what Soup had said about the lamp, or whatever was left of it. The lamp became a limp. Or a lump.

Soup opened the door. "Welcome," he said. "Come on in."

"Yes," said Mrs. Vinson, "as soon as all five of you knock the snow off." She waved a cheery thank-you to Mr. McKell, the man who had hitched his horse to a sleigh. He waved back.

"I'll be back at four o'clock," he said. "Best I go uproad to check if my sister is all right. Happy birthday to your boy."

He, and his horse and sleigh,

turned and left. The sleigh bells went jingling away. Hearing the sleigh bells in October seemed a bit unusual. There were still leaves on the maple trees. The leaves were red and yellow. It made me feel sorry for folks who never got to live right here in Vermont.

The five boys brushed off the snow. Soup's mother watched to see that almost every flake of snow remained outdoors. Where it belonged. Then she smiled. "Welcome to Luther's birthday party," she said.

The boys all looked at each other. Because nobody at school, except of course for Miss Kelly, ever called Soup by the name of Luther. To us, he was Soup.

Ally Tidwell's nose was running.

Soup's mother wiped it, tugged off a boot that was being stubborn, and hung up five sets of soppy wet clothes.

"Once a year," she sighed.

I didn't quite understand what she meant. But my mother would know. Mothers, I had come to believe, all spoke some sort of a secret language, one that only other mothers could understand. For example . . . Whenever my mother is trying to comb my hair, on Sunday morning before church, she talks to my feet. What she says is . . . "Stand still."

Nine

The party started. Soon it was in full blast. Time to play games.

"Okay," said Soup, "let's play Tackle Tag."

"And," I added, "there'll be special prizes for every single winner."

"But not for every married winner," Soup said.

Our first game was Musical

Chairs. Soup's mother had decided to rule out Hog Pile and Rat Race. As it turned out, Musical Chairs was really fun. Mrs. Vinson could play a pump organ. Not very well. Yet her one song, *Rock of Ages,* squawked out good enough to supply all of the background music for a game or two of Musical Chairs. You'll never guess who won the game. I did! I took first prize. It was a dead spider.

Musical Chairs was fun until the chair got broken. After that, we played Pin the Tail on the Donkey. Soup got to go first. He was blindfolded, handed a tail of white cloth with a pin in it, then spun around. So he'd be mixed up. Soup pinned the tail on George Davis. Rolly McGraw found a much larger target, Soup's mother, who was bending over to wipe up a spill. The pin almost stuck her. But she turned around just in time. For the rest of the day, she didn't bend over at all. Even though there were lots of spills. Secretly we changed the name of the game to . . . Pin the Tail on Mrs. Vinson. Ally Tidwell and Stevie Seguso told Soup's mother that they knew two good party games to play.

"What are they?" she asked.

"Pillow Fight," they told her, "and Tug of War."

But we didn't get to try them, because Mrs. Vinson was saying something to Soup, and holding up a warning finger. I didn't hear all she said. Only one word.

"Lamp."

Ten

We pulled taffy. This we could only do in the kitchen, by strict order from Soup's mother. Taffy is fun to pull and even more fun to eat.

We ate taffy, and ate more taffy, until finally Rolly McGraw threw up, and then Mrs. Vinson said it was time for another game to play. Soup and I were chosen to be the first two contestants in the String Chew game.

It starts with a long piece of string, about four feet. The middle of the string holds a gumdrop. We faced each other. One end of the string was in Soup's mouth, the other in mine. The string ran in a level line from his teeth to my teeth. Halfway in between was the prize. An orange gumdrop.

"Go," said Mrs. Vinson.

I chewed. Soup chewed. Inch by inch, we both gnawed closer and closer to the gumdrop. We weren't allowed to use our hands. Only our teeth and lips.

"Faster," yelled Mrs. Vinson.

"Chew faster."

My mouth started to fill with string. All I could see was that one orange gumdrop, and my eyes were crossing. Our faces came closer. And then closer. Each time Soup opened his mouth to chew into another inch of string, I'd bite my end, and pull back. He did the same to me.

It was the longest game of String Chew that was ever played in October in the state of Vermont at an all-boy birthday party for a kid becoming nine during a Saturday-afternoon snowstorm.

Soup won.

I was glad. It was Soup's birthday. All of our prize junk (or junky prizes) got handed out to winners and losers. I gave Soup the present that my mother knitted for him. A pair of bright red wool mittens. Each mitten had a white *S* on it. It stood for Soup.

We ate my mother's ice cream and Soup's mother's cake. The cake had nine candles on it. All in a circle.

"Make a wish," Rolly said.

Closing his eyes, Soup made a wish. Everyone kept silent. Mrs. Vinson smiled. Taking a deep breath, Soup blew out all nine candles (one blew into my ice cream) and we all clapped, and cheered. Best of all, we ate the cake, even though most of it was on the floor. With our mouths full, we sang *Happy Birthday to You.*

It was strange, but Soup's mother wanted neither ice cream nor cake. All she took was four tablets of aspirin. Mrs. Vinson seemed to become much happier when Mr. McKell came back with his horse and sleigh. So the boys got bundled up, thanked Mrs. Vinson for a nice time, and left.

I gave Soup my flat toad. He smiled. I stayed to help Soup clean up the mess. We picked up lots of cake crumbs off the floor, using our tongues.

"Well," I asked Soup, "will you get your birthday wish?"

He looked right at me. "Rob, I already got it." As he punched my shoulder, not hard, I guess I knew what Soup meant . . . that he liked having us Pecks for neighbors.

I felt the same way. A friend is somebody that you give your favorite dead toad to. All the birthday parties in the world couldn't ever be worth more than one very special every-day prize.

A best pal.